Ant Meets the Queen

Jan Burchett and Sara Vogler
Illustrated by Jon Stuart

OXFORD

Chapter 1 – Going underground

The children at Green Bank School had a new project. They were building an eco garden in the corner of the school field. All the children had to take turns digging and planting the flower beds.

One lunchtime Max and his friends took their turn. It was hard work – at least for some of them. Tiger was not digging. He found other ways to get dirty.

"Hey, look what I've found," said Cat, suddenly. Max and Ant put down their spades and went over to where she was standing. "It's a tunnel!"

Ant got on his hands and knees and peered inside. "It's a rabbit hole," he said.

"How can you tell?" asked Max.

"I can see rabbit droppings," said Ant, proudly.

"Err," groaned Cat.

"I wonder where it goes?" said Max.

"Let's find out," whispered Ant.

"What about Tiger?" asked Cat.

They all looked over at Tiger who was practising some tricks with his football.

"I think he's busy," said Max.

When no one was looking, Max, Cat and Ant turned the dials on their watches. They pushed the X and ...

The three micro-friends peered into the rabbit hole. Suddenly it looked very big and very dark.

"Maybe we should have brought Tiger after all," said Ant. "At least he has a torch on his watch."

"Not scared are you?" teased Cat. "It's just a rabbit hole. Rabbits are cute. They eat grass and carrots. What harm can they do?"

"Come on you two," said Max, walking into the darkness.

They set off down the tunnel. Ant started taking some photos using the camera on his watch.

After a while they came to a pile of earth blocking their path.

"Shame we didn't bring our spades," said Ant. "We could have dug our way through."

"We can move this easily with our hands," said Max.

Max was right. Soon they had cleared some of the earth away. They all looked through the gap.

Chapter 2 – The nest

worker ant

"Ants!" cried Max.

"It's a nest," said Ant. "I've always wanted to see inside an ants' nest. This must be one of the main chambers."

"What's a chamber?" asked Max, worried.

"It's like a large room," said Ant.

"I wanted to see a rabbit!" wailed Cat. "Not a load of ants!"

The ants were busy moving little white sacks.

"We've disturbed some of the eggs with our digging," said Ant. "The worker ants are moving them to safety."

"They give me the creeps," said Max, with a shudder.

"It's OK, Max, these are black ants. They don't sting," said Ant. "They might nip a bit though," he added.

"A bit?" said Cat. "Look at those jaws!"

"Let's go," said Max.

But instead of turning to leave, Ant climbed through the hole into the nest.

"Ant!" called out Cat. "What are you doing?"

"Just a quick look," Ant's voice echoed back.

Ant gazed at the ants busily moving their eggs. He took some more photos.

"It's the queen who lays all the eggs," he said. "I wonder where she is?"

Ant wandered off down a narrow passage on the other side of the chamber.

"Come back!" yelled Max.

"We'd better go after him," said Cat.

Max and Cat squeezed through the hole and chased after Ant.

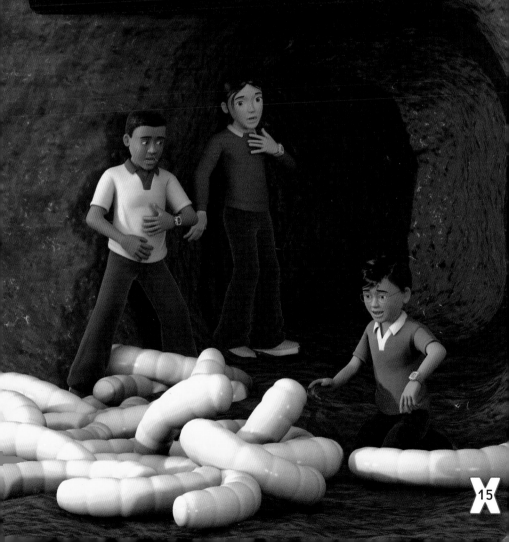

Soon, Ant, followed by Max and Cat, came out into another chamber. It was filled with wriggling creatures.

"Maggots!" said Cat. "Gross."

"Actually they are called larvae," said Ant, excitedly. "They're what the eggs hatch into. The larvae grow up to become ants."

Just then, several worker ants appeared from another tunnel. They were carrying a huge dead caterpillar.

"They look hungry," said Cat, warily.

"They are!" said Ant.

The ants put the caterpillar down and the larvae began to crawl towards it.

"We should leave," insisted Max. "Now!"

"Just one more photo!" said Ant. He lay flat on his belly to get a close up of the larvae eating the caterpillar.

"Ant! Watch out!" cried Max.

Before Ant could move, the line of workers turned and headed straight for him. Together, they picked him up and marched off down a tunnel.

Chapter 3 – The queen

Max and Cat ran down the tunnel after the ants.

"Amazing!" said Ant's voice in the distance. "Did you know ants can carry things ten to twenty times heavier than they are ...?"

"Typical," said Cat, breathlessly. "His life is in danger and he still finds it fascinating!"

The ants carried Ant into a large chamber. In the corner sat the queen ant. She was bigger than the other ants and looked as if she was wearing shiny black armour. All around her the worker ants were busy putting her eggs into piles.

The workers dropped Ant on to the earth.
He pushed himself on to his hands and knees ...
and found himself face to face with the beady eyes
of the queen. She opened her jaws wide.

Ant gulped. He had not planned on getting this
close to her!

Just then, Max and Cat dashed into the chamber.

"Get the ants' attention, Cat," said Max quickly. "And I'll grab our Ant!"

Cat started to shout at the ants and wave her arms. The workers all stopped and turned to look at her. All except the queen. She was too busy looking hungrily at Ant.

Hello, your majesty.

"Take a photo!" shouted Max to Ant.

"I don't think now is a good time ..."

"Just do it," said Max, as he leapt over an ant and raced towards his friend.

Ant took a photo and the flash startled the queen. She reared backwards away from the light.

Max grabbed Ant's arm and pulled him to his feet.
"Can we please get out of here now?" said Max.

"Er, yes," said Ant, shaken. "I think that would be
a good idea."

They both ran after Cat who had ducked into a
nearby tunnel.

Chapter 4 – Time to go!

The children scrambled along the tunnel. Behind them they could hear thundering feet as the worker ants followed them.

"Quick!" said Ant urgently. "They'll be sending out chemical signals to the rest of the colony saying the nest is under attack. Every ant in the place will be after us."

The tunnel began to climb. Slipping and sliding, the children tried to get away. There were ants close behind them.

"They're catching up," wailed Cat.

They came to a side tunnel. It was full of ants coming towards them. They tried to go forwards, but ahead of them the tunnel was completely blocked.

The ants surrounded them. They started to advance on the micro-friends, like an army. They snapped their jaws fiercely.

"What are we going to do now?" wailed Cat.

"Any suggestions, Ant?" said Max.

Then, just as everything seemed hopeless, there was a loud rumbling noise behind them. The rumbling got louder. The ants turned and fled down the tunnel.

"It's an earthquake!" cried Ant.

"The tunnel's collapsing," yelled Max.

But it was not an earthquake and the tunnel did not collapse. Instead, a big furry nose poked out from the earth next to them. Then a head appeared.

"A rabbit!" said Ant.

"It's so cute," said Cat.

The rabbit sniffed the air then thumped the ground with its foot. It bolted back the way it had come, back up a different tunnel towards ...

"Daylight!" cried Max.

Max, Cat and Ant scrambled through the hole the rabbit had made and ran towards the tunnel entrance. Behind them, the ants scuttled back to their nest and their angry queen.

"There you are!" cried Tiger, when he saw the others again. They were back to their normal size. "Where have you been?"

"We've been underground!" said Ant. "We saw an ants' nest and it was really cool!"

"Cool?" said Max. "You were nearly eaten by the queen!"

"You've been on a micro-adventure without me?" said Tiger, sadly.

"Don't worry, Tiger," said Cat. "Ant took lots of photos!"

Retell the story . . .

Find out more ...

For more underground
adventures read ...
A NASTI Surprise

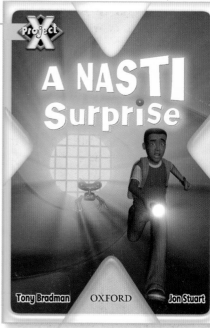

To find out more
about ants read ...
Ants at Home

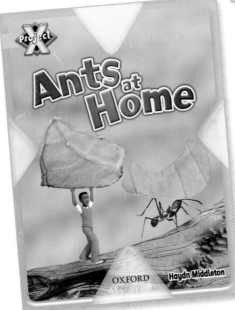